Inside the dollshouse.

Inside the dollshouse

Calligraphy & Illustration
by Hilary Unwin.

Shepheard-Walwyn

First published 1989 by
Shepheard-Walwyn (Publishers) Ltd,
Suite 34, 26 Charing Cross Rd,
London WC2H 0DH

ISBN 0 85683 121 2

Printed & Bound in Great Britain by
The Roundwood Press, Kineton, Warwick.

For
Jamie & Sienna
the inheritors
of the
dollshouse

THE two tiny lavender dolls sat with their backs against the wooden calligraphy box. It was a beautiful box, hand carved, with inset panels of delicately woven, bright coloured embroidery and it stood on the second shelf of an equally pretty arched wicker unit where both the dolls and the box were much admired.

THE shelves of the wicker unit contained all manner of bric-a-brac, numerous books on a wide variety of crafts, scented pot-pourri, herb sachets and several other dolls. A beautifully dressed clown sat on the top shelf, looking exceptionally sad, but two smaller clowns, with smiling faces, climbed around the frame, clasping the unruly offspring of an enormous spider plant. Lower down sat a wooden artist figure, his rigidly positioned arms set in an awkward posture, his face blank, his unseeing eyes turned to the shelf below where a china castle  containing coloured pencils served as an ornamental book end.

MONGST these surroundings, the two little dolls should have been very happy, and indeed when the dolls had first arrived they had considered themselves to be extremely fortunate: how nice to sit amongst such pretty things, with interesting companions of superior quality, instead of being squashed in the bottom of a dark toy box, along with a lot of riff-raff from Hong-Kong.

MELISSA at three and three-quarter inches was slightly taller than Oliver and therefor felt herself to be the more mature of the two dolls. She frequently reminded Oliver of their good fortune and when he complained of an occasional stiffness, from sitting with his back permanently arched on the calligraphy box, she would admonish him with a sympathetic glance toward the wooden artists model.

HOWEVER Melissa's content‑
ment was shattered by the
appearance of the dolls house.
The dolls had actually arrived
the very same Christmas as the house,
but as the latter had been packed in a
large flat box and was no more than
numerous sheets of dull plywood, the
dolls had, had no suspicions that it
would become the mansion it now
appeared.

THE dolls had watched
with interest as the pieces of
wood assembled to the shape
of a house, but still many months
had gone by before it had be‑
come the desirable detached
residence it now appeared, boas‑
ting eight rooms all papered
with miniature papers
of the most intricate de‑
tail, from the tiny delft
tiles in the kitchen to the
pictures of Alice and the white rabbit
in the attic nursery.

T was at this stage that Melissa decided that the house was intended for her and Oliver. There was no furniture as yet, but the window seats were absolutely perfect

everything
was
going
to be just
the
right
size for
the
two tiny
dolls

MELISSA could visualize herself languidly, lounging on the blue padded silk in the drawing room and the bedroom was obviously going to be furnished in pink, her favourite colour. Already pink drapes hung at the windows with lovely frilled cushions plumped on the window seats. "Oh", thought Melissa, "It would be heaven to live in such a house."

BUT weeks went by and although the dolls house now had a permanent position in the opposite corner of the room, Melissa and Oliver were no nearer to being its occupants than the smiling clowns or the wooden artists figure.

Slowly, beautiful pieces of dark, mahogany furniture arrived, first the master bedroom came alive with a wonderful double bed, Melissa saw the thick striped mattress and embroidered sheets, going under the eiderdown, and thought how comfortable she would be in such a bed. There were tiny bedside tables with minute brass candlesticks, although the dolls knew that the house actually had real working lights, for Melissa and Oliver had watched in amazement as the tiny lights, in their pretty shades, had shone brightly in every room

THE bedroom also contained a dressing table with a big ornate mirror. Melissa had never seen her reflection and she longed to sit infront of that mirror, using the tiny brush and comb that were placed on a dainty painted tray alongside pretty perfume bottles, a soft pink powder puff, and even a tiny black leather bible. On one occasion the dresser drawers had been left open and  Melissa had seen that they were full of tiny pieces of lace and frippery.

A small round stool sat in front of the dressing table, topped by a pink satin cushion. Melissa was not at all sure that she would be able to balance on such a stool, but she told herself she would worry about that later.

ACROSS the landing from the bedroom was another beautiful room with panelled walls and long tasselled drapes. The furnishings and rugs were all in shades of old gold and an Adams fireplace housed a log fire complete with fire irons and an impressive brass fender, but it was when a spectacular grand piano appeared in the centre of the room that even Oliver itched to try his hand at a piano concerto.

He had never played a piano, but he was sure it wouldn't be too difficult, there was music on the piano and on a music stand, so if he couldn't manage the piano he would play the violin which lay with its bow on a multi-cushioned velvet sofa, awaiting just such a musical talent as Oliver was sure that he undoubtedly possessed.

DOWNSTAIRS the victorian parlour was also fully furnished, each piece of furniture fitting perfectly with its surroundings. But Melissa was puzzled, on the foot stool, sat a tiny piece of knitting, half worked, a pencil sketch with ready sharpened pencil lay on the window seat and on the bureau was a half written letter with a desk blotter that had clearly been used for much previous correspondence. The little doll was absolutely sure that no other dolls lived in the house, nothing was ever moved and the biscuits sitting with an empty tea cup were never eaten, but who would have made these things? There were carrier bags and boxes in the bedroom as if someone had just returned from a shopping trip... Melissa became quite vexed, it was to be her house, she didn't want anyone leaving their possessions lying about, she would soon put a stop to it as soon as she moved in.

BUT when would she move in? Another Christmas had come and gone, and still the dolls sat on the wicker unit, while the beautiful house, looked more and more like the home of Melissa's dreams.

In the past few months the kitchen had taken shape, an oak dresser held a wide variety of cooking utensils, there was an old fashioned butler sink on brick piers and a lovely black lead range and again the mysterious signs of occupation. In the oven was a cherry-pie cooked and ready to eat. Whilst on the stove some one was actually cooking breakfast and yet the sausage and egg were never served, although the kitchen table was permanently laid and ready for breakfast.

T was all very strange and Melissa tried to make Oliver understand the full implications, but the boys enthusiasm enlivened by the music room had since waned.

 OLIVER did not share his sisters fascination with the dining room cabinet or the circular dining table. He showed no interest in the set of wine goblets or the upholstered dining chairs.

HE did have a certain curiosity about the tiny silver bird that sat on a swing inside a tall brass cage, but Oliver felt that if the house was meant for them, one day he would be able to examine it all, but until that day came he would be perfectly happy with his life on the wicker unit.

OWEVER Oliver's attitude changed with the arrival of the nursery furniture. Melissa greatly admired the brightly coloured patchwork quilt and the oval rugs with numbers and letters worked in to the design, but Oliver was fascinated by the toys.

 A black and red train set, ran right under the bed. There were teddy bears, soldiers,  a clown, a clockwork mouse and a golliwog all stuffed into a bright red toy box. An incomplete jig-saw showed a picture of a steam train and Oliver's fingers itched to fit the final pieces

 just as he longed to replace the jiggling jack-in-the-box and then watch him jump back out on his wobbly spring.

THE toy cupboard was packed with boxes, Oliver could see a lovely red drum and a set of building blocks a spinning top and a trumpet, so many toys and all just the right size for him to play with.

MELISSA felt impatience mounting, this really was not fair, beside the house being left unoccupied for all this time, who ever owned the house really ought to keep it a little tidier. In the nursery all the cupboard doors

and drawers were left wide open, it really was not good enough; the little doll told herself she would soon sort out all the mess, just as soon as she could get aross the room and inside the house.

ow that Oliver's interest in the dolls house was revived, the two tiny dolls planned together to devise a way in which they might get into the dolls house. Yet another Christmas was approaching, a tiny tree decorated with lights and with presents piled underneath had been set in the dolls house dining room, perhaps they would move in for Christmas, "Oh, how wonderful that would be!"

MELISSA had decided against the pink bedroom she would live in the attic nursery with Oliver. She planned  to teach him his letters at the blackboard, one of the many books was sure to show her how. Although how Melissa would read, since she didn't know her own letters remains a complete mystery.

STILL Melissa was confident that she was a particularly clever and superior little doll, destined to occupy a very desirable resid-ence and just as soon as she became the owner-occupier she would manage not only the lessons, but the whole house, she would see that it was all kept neat and tidy, no more open cupboards, half finished work or partly prepared food dishes.

WHY Melissa could see right into the sewing room at the very top of the house and someone had started  cutting out fabric, presumably to make a dress, the pattern for which lay on the sewing machine, and left all the cuttings and scraps lying on the carpet, even the scissors hadn't been replaced in the wicker sewing basket that lay open on the floor amidst all the muddle.

CHRISTMAS came and went, many visitors had been to look at the dolls house and had admired the beautifully designed rugs which were the latest additions. One or two people had even walked across the room and held Melissa and Oliver, but no one had thought to take the two little dolls to the house where they might sit on the perfect size chairs or play amongst the toys in the attic nursery.

THAT had been Melissa's last hope for she had eventually realized that the house had not been made for her. She had known for certain when she had seen the daintiest pair of ladies slippers abandoned on the bathroom floor. Melissa had looked down at her solid wooden legs and she knew that if ever a doll did move in, it would be a doll with tiny china feet and golden hair not pink wool locks like her own.

THE truth was very painful to Melissa and with its dawning her whole attitude to her life changed. For four years she had sat on the wicker unit longing for the day that she would move into the house, now that she feared that day would never come she became so discontented her whole personality was affected.

SOON poor Oliver was afraid to speak to his sister, he had tried to explain to her that although he still sometimes looked across the room at the toys in the nursery with admiration, he felt that they should accept the inevitable and make the most of their life as it was. He even tried to remind her how superior she had once thought the wicker unit but Melissa
COULD NOT
WOULD NOT
come to terms with the empty house and became, really quite unbearable to live with.

EVENTUALLY a day came when lots of little girls were visiting the house together. Melissa guessed it was a birthday party, and at one time the little doll would have been happy just to watch the children with the presents and balloons, but now her pleasure in everything was spoilt by a constant air of discontent, so that she hardly noticed the colourful cards or the candlelit cake

MELISSA was thus caught completely by surprise when she was picked up by a small girl and carried to the dolls house. First she was sat in the nursery rocking chair, then tucked into the wonderfully comfortable bed and finally rested on the beautiful blue window seat in the drawing-room, she could hardy believe that, after all this time, this was really happening to her.

MELISSA puffed up her lavender filled body with pride, she felt every inch the lady of the manor, and as the little girls all looked at her inside the dolls house, she imagined that they would all admire her and envy her, her beautiful home. Actually the children had begun to lose interest in the house and soon started to play games.

MELISSA prayed desperately that no one would remember that she was still in the dolls house, she looked around at the marvellous room, now she could truly appreciate the detailed pattern on the carpet, the delicate embroidery on the cushions and the ornate cornice on the ceiling.

IF only the little girls would leave her there, she didn't care about Oliver, she didn't care about any of her old friends, she didn't care about anything, just as long as she could stay in the beautiful house.

AND stay she did, in fact Melissa stayed on the window seat for many months. Somehow the little doll had imagined that once inside the house some magic would enable her to examine all the treasures that she had admired from across the room, instead she was as immobile as she had been on the wicker unit and she was lonely.

MELISSA was surprised to find how much she missed Oliver. She could not see across the room to where he sat with his back against the calligraphy box but she could visualize him along with the smiling clowns and the wooden artists model. It was strange that Melissa should now feel envy for the wooden figure perched so awkwardly on a too small chair, when she had previously, always felt such deep sympathy for him. It would seem that Melissa, was a little doll, who was prone to feel envy and discontent whatever her situation.

THE fact was that the little doll had gradually slumped down into the window seat and was now extremely uncomfortable herself and amazingly she was also unbelievably bored by her luxurious surroundings. Melissa no longer admired the beautiful cushions, the buttons on the blue padded silk dug into her soft lavender body. The pattern on the carpet was so familiar that she knew the exact number of roses within the design, and she had stared for so long at the family portraits framed on the wall that they now seemed to look back at her with supercillious smiles.

ON the wicker unit the little doll had been able to see the entire room, but in the dolls house her whole world was contained in one miniature drawing room and consequently she became irrationally irritated by the unmoving clock while the biscuits on the china plate made her feel constantly hungry.

DURING those months Melissa learnt some important lessons that she would never have learnt at the easel with Oliver. She learnt that a beautiful house didn't necessarily make a wonderful home, that possessions gave no lasting pleasure if their acquisition was intended to create envy, and perhaps the most important lesson, that family and friends were the greatest treasures she would ever possess.

EVERYDAY that Melissa was on her own in the dolls house made her more aware how very foolish she had been. Poor little doll, she had been so desperate to move into the house she had ceased to think about anything else, including the benifits of her old life, and now that she realized how silly she had been she was afraid that it was too late and she would never get back to Oliver and her old friends on the wicker unit.

BUT fortunately Melissa had been absolutely right about one thing. The dolls house had never been intended for her, and so when I saw her slumped on the window seat I knew straight away that she didn't belong in those surroundings.

I HAD made the dolls house as a model house, not intended for dolls at all, and certainly not for a doll like Melissa. To me she looked so out of place I am surprised that I didn't notice her before. Still maybe that is just as well, it often takes a lifetime to learn the lessons that Melissa learnt during her months in the dolls house and now when I see her sitting with Oliver in her old home on the wicker unit she  looks a much happier and wiser little doll.

HE house still has no occupants, not even a dainty china doll with golden hair, so I will have to admit to being the one who made the rooms so untidy, thus causing poor house-proud Melissa so much distress.

THE disorder was deliberate because although I love my miniature house and spent many years making it as perfect as possible, I do think that all houses, however grand should have a lived in feel to them,

.... don't you?